Bustop the Cat and Mrs. Lin
By Amy Reichert

Illustrated by Donna Ryan

ISBN 1-880812-12-6

5 7 9 10 8 6 4

Published by Storytellers Ink
Seattle, Washington

Printed in the United States of America

Dedication

To Mom with love.   - A.R.

Contents

Chapter I
Mrs. Lin Rides to Town

Every morning Mrs. Lin caught the Number 10 bus.

"Good morning, Gus," she'd say cheerfully as she paid the driver her fare.

"Humph!" Gus would grumble back. He was never in a very good mood.

Mrs. Lin liked to sit in the front of the bus so she could smile at all the other passengers as they boarded. She always hoped someone friendly would sit next to her so they could have a nice long chat.

But that didn't usually happen.

"A whole bus full of people," Mrs. Lin would sigh, "and not a soul to talk to." Then she'd shake her head sadly and settle back in her seat for the long ride to town in silence.

Mrs. Lin worked as a switchboard operator for a small company downtown.

"Smith, Hanson and Ross. Good Morning! May I help you?"

"Get me Mr. Smith on the line. Pronto!"

"Tell Mr. Hanson we'll be delivering his grand piano at 2 p.m. precisely. Please don't keep us waiting."

"Singing telegram for Mr. Ross. Happy birthday to you...."

Mrs. Lin answered the phone over and over again, all day long. But the phone was always for someone else. Nobody ever called to talk to her.

Chapter II
A New Friend

In the evening, Mrs. Lin returned to the apartment where she lived alone. She quickly turned on the lights, music, and the television, and started cooking her supper on the stove. Soon her home was bright and cheerful, full of happy sounds and mouth-watering smells.

But there was one thing missing. There was no one for Mrs. Lin to share it all with, and sometimes she felt very lonely.

One morning Mrs. Lin caught the Number 10 bus, as usual. It was a bleak winter's day. The wind was cold and biting.

"Cold enough to freeze a bear in its tracks. What do you think, Gus?" she asked.

"Humph!" Gus grumbled back, sounding a bit like a bear himself.

Mrs. Lin took her favorite seat by the window and smiled at the other passengers as they boarded.
But no one smiled back.
Mrs. Lin got ready for another long, lonely ride into town.

As the Number 10 pulled up to a stop, it began to rain, softly at first, then harder and harder. People stood in line huddling, waiting impatiently to board the bus.

"Poor souls," thought Mrs. Lin. "Oh well, they'll all be warm and dry soon enough."

She started to look away when something caught her eye. At first Mrs. Lin thought someone had left behind a sweater.

But then it moved. "Goodness gracious, it's a cat!" she cried. "Poor thing, it's so thin, and soaking wet. Why, something must be done!"

Mrs. Lin quickly grabbed her lunch bag and headed for the door.

"Just where do you think you're going?" shouted Gus as she climbed down the stairs of the bus.

"I'm sorry," Mrs. Lin called as she rushed towards the bus stop bench. "Please don't leave without me. I'll be right back."

The rain was pouring down now, and Mrs. Lin had neither a hood nor an umbrella. By the time she reached the bus stop bench she was a sorry sight, but not half as sorry as the cat crouched there.

It was fur and bones, and not much more. The poor thing was clearly half starved to death.

BEEP BEEP!!! BEEP BEEP!!!

Gus honked impatiently on the horn.

"Are you coming, or not?" he yelled.

"Just a minute, Gus," Mrs. Lin shouted back. Quickly, she pulled the meat out of her sandwich.

"Now you eat all of this," she told the cat. "If you're here tomorrow, I'll have more for you then."

Back on the bus, Mrs. Lin barely noticed the dirty looks she was getting from Gus and the other passengers. For outside her window the sun was peeking through and the hungry cat was gobbling down her meal.

From that day on Mrs. Lin always packed two lunches, one for herself and one for her new little friend.

At first the cat was shy and wary. Sometimes Mrs. Lin didn't see it at all. But she always left food behind anyway, and it was always gone the next day.

Soon the cat grew to trust her.

Chapter III
Time Together and Time Apart

"We need to find a good name for you," Mrs. Lin told the cat one day.

"How about Scrawny? Or Hungry? Or Bones?"

The cat stared back at her blankly.

"You're right," said Mrs. Lin. "They're true, but not very kind." She looked around for a better idea and saw the bus stop sign.

"That's it!" she cried. "Bustop! It's where we met, and where we see each other every day. Why, Bustop! It's the perfect name."

Bustop began to purr softly.

On the weekends Mrs. Lin didn't work, so she spent most of her time with Bustop.

They watched birds together.

They had picnic lunches.

They napped on the bus stop
bench.

They were very happy—until
it came time to leave.

"I wish I could take you home with me," Mrs. Lin would sigh, "but no pets are allowed where I live. You understand Bustop, don't you?"

Bustop, of course, didn't understand, and sometimes tried to follow Mrs. Lin onto the bus.

But Gus was always too quick with the doors.

BANG!!! SLAM!!! CLANK!!!

Then he'd point to a sign above him that read: "NO FOOD—NO ANIMALS ON BOARD!"

"Don't be sad, Bustop," Mrs. Lin would cry as the bus pulled away from the curb. "Remember, I'll be back to see you tomorrow."

But goodbyes were never easy—for either of them.

Gradually the days grew longer and warmer, and winter turned into spring. By now everyone on the Number 10 route had made friends with Bustop too.

There was Mrs. Cohen, the chef, who liked to bring Bustop treats, and Doctor Jordan, a people doctor, who seemed to know a lot about cats. The twins liked to leave little toys for Bustop near the bench, and everyone else on the Number 10 bus always smiled now and asked, "How's the cat today, Mrs. Lin?"

"Never healthier, never happier," Mrs. Lin was always happy to say.

And it was true. Bustop was thriving. Her coat was thick and glossy. Her eyes were bright and clear. And she was getting bigger and friendlier by the day.

Chapter IV
A Big Surprise

One morning Mrs. Lin arrived for her usual visit, but Bustop wasn't there.

"Bustop," she called up and down the street.

"Bustop," she yelled into the bushes and trees, but Bustop didn't appear. Mrs. Lin began to fear the worst.

"Meow," suddenly a voice came from the bushes nearby. "Meow, meow, meow."

Mrs. Lin poked through the branches and leaves, then cried out with relief and joy.

"Why, Bustop. I thought you were lost, or injured, or sick! But kittens—well, it never occured to me!"

Then she laughed, and cried, and missed her bus, but was too happy to care.

Almost everyone on the Number 10 bus wanted one of Bustop's kittens after having seen them.

"Look how cute they are, all lined up in a row."

"I want the orange fuzzy one, sitting in the middle."

"Can we have the striped one, Mrs. Lin? Can we, please?" begged the twins.

Mrs. Lin thought the kittens should have good homes, and she was certain Bustop would agree. She was therefore very choosy, and asked lots of questions before giving any away.

"Are you really going to play with this kitten," she'd inquire, "and feed it, have it vaccinated, and spayed or neutered? It's easy enough to love a little kitten. Are you going to feel the same way about a big old cat?"

Eventually all the kittens found good homes, and only Bustop was left.

"I know what it's like to be old and alone, but don't worry, Bustop," Mrs. Lin reassured her friend.

"As long as we have each other, we'll be just fine." And they were, until one day....

Chapter V
Crisis

RING! RING! RING! RING! The little alarm clock rattled on the bedside table. Mrs. Lin moaned.

She felt awful. Her head throbbed, her throat ached, and she felt even worse when she tried to get out of bed.

"Now don't you worry about a thing," her office told her when she called to say she wouldn't be in. "We'll manage without you. Just relax and take care of yourself."

Mrs. Lin just couldn't relax or stop worrying. Smith, Hanson and Ross might be able to take care of itself, but what about poor Bustop?

"What will she do when I don't show up?" she wondered. "What if she follows the bus into traffic?"

Late that afternoon there was a knock at her door.

It was Mrs. Cohen carrying a big pot.

"Everybody on the bus was concerned when you didn't show up this morning," she explained. "When they called your office and found out you were sick, I decided to bring you some chicken soup."

Mrs. Lin didn't know what to say. Bustop, of course, had many friends on the bus, but Mrs. Lin had never really thought of them as her friends too. Now she knew she was wrong.

"By the way," added Mrs. Cohen, "Bustop is just fine. The twins shared their tuna fish sandwich with her this morning and someone else gave her a cup of milk. We'll take care of her while you're away, I promise."

Mrs Lin smiled and gave her a hug.

The next afternoon Mrs. Cohen came back, this time with Dr. Jordan.

"I just wanted to make sure that you didn't have anything serious," he said after giving her a thorough exam. "But it's nothing that a bit of rest and," he added with a wink, "a lot of Mrs. Cohen's home cooking won't cure."

The following afternoon the twins came to visit, bringing drawings and decorated cards.

Dr. Jordan called to see how she was.

And Mrs. Cohen brought a hot casserole and rolls.

By the weekend Mrs. Lin was well enough to visit Bustop, and by Monday she was back on the bus again.

"I don't know what Bustop and I would have done without all your help," she told everyone on the bus. "No one could hope for better friends than you."

The Number 10 bus cheered.

Chapter VI
A New Start

That evening Mrs. Cohen called.

"I've just found out," she told Mrs. Lin excitedly, "that the apartment next door to mine is becoming vacant. Why don't you take it?" she urged her friend. "It would be so wonderful to have you as a neighbor, and since pets are allowed, you can bring Bustop too!"

Mrs. Lin was silent for a moment.

"I'd love nothing more than to be your neighbor," sighed Mrs. Lin, "and to give Bustop a proper home. But I just can't afford the expense."

"Nonsense!" said Mrs. Cohen. "My apartment building is the best deal in town, and as far as the actual moving goes, I'm sure we can round up a few people to help."

Mrs. Lin decided to move. Early on the morning of moving day, Mrs. Lin heard a knock at her door. It was Mrs. Cohen, and all of her other friends from the Number 10 bus. Someone had a truck for the big furniture. Everyone else helped in different ways.

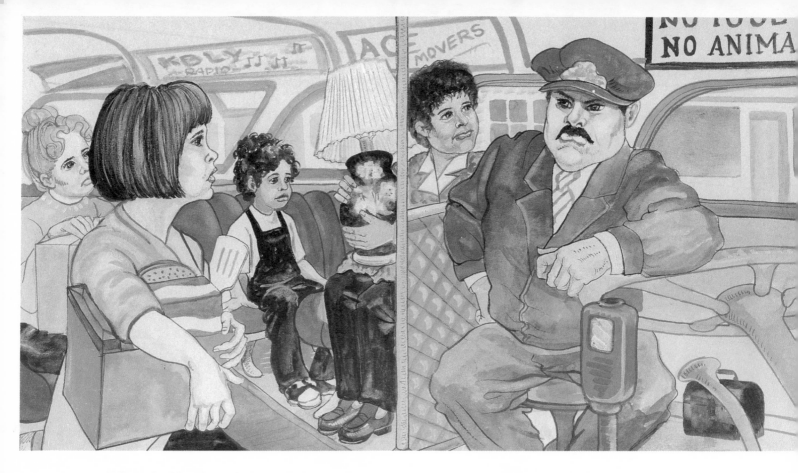

When the Number 10 bus pulled up to the curb, Mrs. Lin was the first to climb aboard.

"Good morning, Gus," she said with a happy smile. "I'm moving today."

"Humph!" said Gus, as usual, so Mrs. Lin sat down.

Bustop was waiting at the bench when the Number 10 bus arrived. Mrs. Lin looked first at Gus and then at the "NO FOOD—NO ANIMALS ON BOARD!" sign.

Everyone on the bus held their breath.

"Well, what are you waiting for?" Gus finally grumbled. "Are you going to get that cat, or not?"

Mrs. Lin quickly brought Bustop on board. Then Gus left the route and pulled right up to Mrs. Lin's new apartment building, parked the bus and let everybody off.

"Thank you, Gus!" whispered Mrs. Lin. "I always knew you had a heart."

"Humph!" said Gus, but Mrs. Lin didn't hear; she was already half-way out the door.

Mrs. Lin gave Bustop a tour of the apartment.

"Well, Bustop," she asked, "what do you think of our new home?" Bustop began to purr loudly.

Everybody laughed and cheered,

"Hooray for Bustop and Mrs. Lin!"

Mrs. Lin turned to her friends and shouted,

"Hooray for everyone on the Number 10 bus!"